™.

Detective Duckworth to the Rescue

By Annie Cobb • Illustrated by Kathy Wilburn

Silver Press

*Produced by Chardiet Unlimited, Inc. and Daniel Weiss Associates, Inc.
33 West 17th Street, New York, NY 10011*

*Educational Consultant:
Dr. Priscilla Lynch*

*GOING PLACES™ is a trademark of Daniel Weiss Associates, Inc.
and Chardiet Unlimited, Inc.*

*Published by Silver Press, a division of
Silver Burdett Press, Inc., Simon & Schuster, Inc.
Prentice Hall Bldg., Englewood Cliffs, NJ 07632
For information address: Silver Press.*

*Printed in the United States of America
10 9 8 7 6 5 4 3 2 1*

Library of Congress Cataloging-in-Publication Data

*Cobb, Annie
Detective Duckworth to the Rescue/written by Annie Cobb;
illustrated by Kathy Wilburn
p.   cm.—(Going places)
Summary: The inimitable Detective Duckworth solves The Case of
The Missing Eggs with the help of maps, logical thinking and his
friends in the woods.
1. Going—Juvenile literature. [1. Going] I. Wilburn, Kathy, ill. II.
Title. III. Series: Going places
(Englewood Cliffs, N.J.)*

*ISBN 0-671-70394-3 (LSB)
ISBN 0-671-70398-6 (trade)*

Detective Duckworth was finishing lunch when
Postmaster Crow arrived with a special delivery letter.
Duckworth opened the envelope and read the letter.

Dear Duckworth,
Please come quickly.
Something terrible has happened.
Your cousin,
Mrs. Duck

Duckworth wasted no time. He packed his flight bag with a little glass vial, his clue box, and a map of the woods.

Then he went outside and flew towards the woods where Mrs. Duck lived.

Ten minutes later he landed near Mrs. Duck's house at the west end of Beaver Pond. He knew immediately what the trouble was—nobody was home.

"I see," cried Duckworth. "It's the Case of the Missing Mrs.! I should have known."

Then he noticed that there was mud all around
Mrs. Duck's house. He took out the tiny glass bottle
and filled it with mud. He put the bottle in his clue
box.

Suddenly he heard a noise. Someone was coming.
He ducked behind a tree and waited. Who could it
be?

It was Squirrel.

"Hold it right there!" said Duckworth, jumping out from behind the tree.

"Hi, Detective Duckworth," said Squirrel. "Mrs. Duck sent me here to find you. She forgot to tell you that she moved to Mrs. Goose's house this morning."

"Aha!" said Duckworth. "The Case of the Missing Mrs. is solved!"

Duckworth and Squirrel walked over to the ferry.

"All aboard for East End!" called Beaver.
Duckworth and Squirrel hopped aboard.

Beaver pointed to the big rock on the northern shore of Beaver Pond. There sat Groundhog with his fishing pole.

"Wonder how many fish Groundhog has caught," said Beaver. "Brought him over on the ferry from East End this morning. He's been fishing ever since."

When Duckworth and Squirrel arrived at Mrs.
Goose's house on the east end of Beaver Pond, Mrs.
Duck raced out to meet them.

"I'm so glad you're here," said Mrs. Duck. "I need
a detective. My eggs have disappeared!"

"It's the Case of the Disappearing Eggs," cried
Duckworth. "I should have known."

Suddenly Duckworth saw something round and blue in the grass. He picked it up. It was a blueberry.

"Very interesting!" cried Duckworth.

"But it's just an ordinary blueberry," said Squirrel.

"Yes," said Duckworth, "but there are no blueberry bushes here." And he put it into his clue box.

Then they all went inside and Mrs. Duck told
Duckworth the whole story.

"You see, I had to move because of the mud," she
explained. "Mrs. Goose was kind enough to invite
me to stay with her. I packed my suitcase and I put
my eggs in a basket. I even put a little pink blanket
over them to keep them warm. Then I put the
suitcase in my little wagon and I set the basket right
next to it. I didn't take the ferry. I walked along the
path to Mrs. Goose's house. When I got here, the
basket was gone."

"We were so frantic, we even turned the wagon
over and jumped on it," said Mrs. Goose. "But still
no eggs."

Duckworth took out his map of the woods. He opened it up and lay it down on the table.

"Now then, Mrs. Duck," said Duckworth. "Show me the path you took from your house to Mrs. Goose's house."

Mrs. Duck showed Duckworth the path she took. Can you find it?

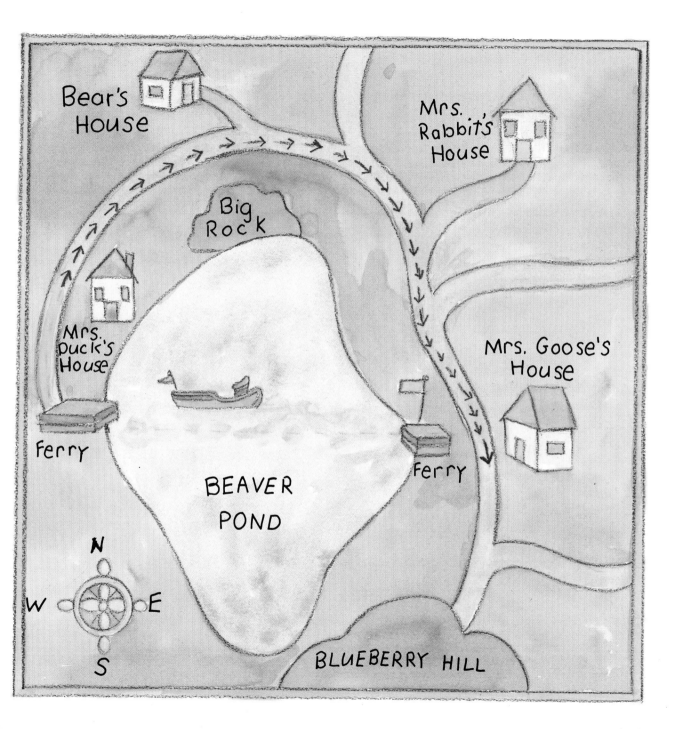

"Did you see anyone along the way?" asked Duckworth.

"Yes," said Mrs. Duck. "I saw Groundhog. He was fishing on the big rock. And there was someone else too...a fox. I didn't recognize him. He said he was going to visit Bear. He was carrying a very large suitcase."

"A very large suitcase? Hmmmm," said Duckworth. "I should have known."

Mrs. Duck looked at the map. She pointed to the spot where she had seen Groundhog and where she had seen the fox.

This is where she saw

This is where she saw Groundhog.

Bear's House

Mrs. Rabbits House

Big Rock

Mrs. Duck's House

"Did you see anyone else?" asked Duckworth.

"As a matter of fact, I did," said Mrs. Duck.
"I saw Mrs. Rabbit and her two children, Mibs
and Dibs. She was going home to her new house."

Mrs. Duck showed Duckworth the place on the
map where she saw Mrs. Rabbit. Duckworth marked
it.

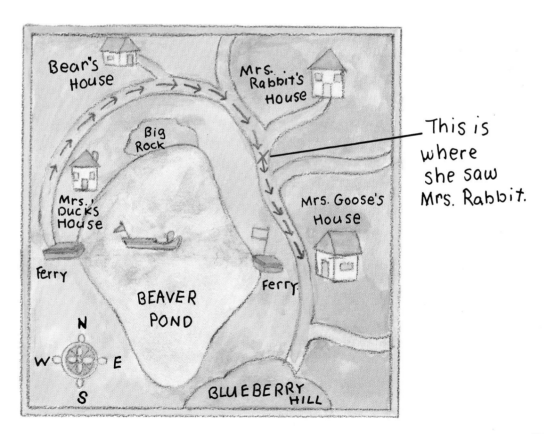

Suddenly Duckworth gasped. He was staring at a pair of muddy boots by Mrs. Goose's door.

Duckworth took out the bottle of mud he had collected at Mrs. Duck's house. He compared the mud in the bottle with the mud on the boots. It was an exact match.

"Now," said Duckworth to Squirrel, "as soon as we find out who wore these boots today, we will have solved The Case of the... The Case of the..."

"The Case of the Muddy Boots?" asked Squirrel.

Just then Mrs. Duck looked up from the map. "What are you doing with my boots?" she asked.

"Aha!" cried Duckworth. "The Case of the Muddy Boots is solved."

"I think it is time to visit Fox and Bear," said
Duckworth.

When they got to Bear's house, Bear was very
happy to see them.

"I'm sorry I don't have a place for everybody to
sit," apologized Bear. "I only have one chair."

"Please give it to Mrs. Duck," said Duckworth.

Then Duckworth spied the very large suitcase in the corner of the room.

"May I look inside?" he asked.

"I can't open it right now," said Fox.

"I see," said Duckworth. And then he whispered to Squirrel, "I need you to find a way to get Fox out of the house for a while."

Squirrel went outside.

As he was looking around for a way to get Fox out of the house, he tripped and fell into a deep hole.

"Help! Help!" cried Squirrel.

Fox and Bear and Mrs. Duck and Mrs. Goose all came running.

Now was Duckworth's chance! He walked quickly over to the very large suitcase and opened it.

There was a brand-new chair, with a note—

> For Bear,
> Surprise!
> From your friend,
> > Fox.

"Aha! The reason Fox did not want me to open his suitcase was that he didn't want Bear to see the surprise inside," thought Duckworth.

When he went outside, he saw Fox pulling Squirrel out of a very deep hole. "Fox did not take the basket," Duckworth said to Squirrel.

"Now it is time for us to visit Mrs. Rabbit."

As they walked along, Squirrel asked, "What about Groundhog? Are we going to visit him?"

"Groundhog did not take the basket," said Duckworth.

"How do you know?" asked Squirrel.

"Just look at the map!" said Duckworth.

He held up the map for Squirrel to see.

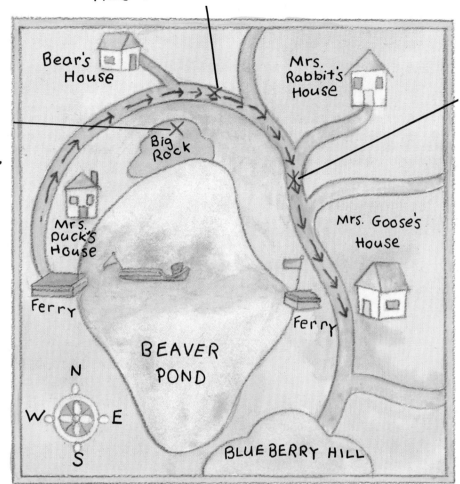

This is where she saw Fox.

This is where she saw Mrs. Rabbit.

his is here he saw oundhog.

Bear's House

Mrs. Rabbit's House

Big Rock

Mrs. Duck's House

Ferry

Mrs. Goose's House

Ferry

BEAVER POND

N
W — E
S

BLUEBERRY HILL

"Beaver took Groundhog on the ferry to West End this morning," explained Duckworth. "Groundhog took the ferry from the east end to the west end and walked to the rock on the northern shore of Beaver Pond. Whoever took the basket came from Blueberry Hill."

Duckworth took the blueberry out of the clue box. "Here is the first clue—a blueberry, found on the grass next to Mrs. Goose's house."

"There are no blueberry bushes there," said Squirrel.

"But," said Duckworth, "there are blueberry bushes on Blueberry Hill. Whoever took the basket of eggs dropped a blueberry into Mrs. Duck's wagon. That means whoever took the basket was on Blueberry Hill this morning."

Soon, Duckworth and Squirrel arrived at
Mrs. Rabbit's house. She welcomed them inside.
Her children Mibs and Dibs were playing in the
living room.

"Children, bring a pillow for Mrs. Duck," she said.

Instantly, Mibs and Dibs turned up, each holding a
pillow.

"Two pillows!" cried Mrs. Duck. "How nice."

"Children, bring a plate of cookies for our guests,"
said Mrs. Rabbit.

Instantly, Mibs and Dibs turned up, each holding a
plate of cookies.

"Two plates of cookies!" squealed Squirrel. "Wow!"

Suddenly Duckworth cried out: "Aha! The Case of
the Disappearing Eggs...is solved!"

Everyone stared at Duckworth in astonishment.

Duckworth took out the map of the woods. He opened it so everyone could see. "If you look at the map, you will see that Mrs. Rabbit came home from Blueberry Hill." It seems that Mrs. Rabbit was picking blueberries this morning and brought them home in a...in a..."

"Basket!" said Mrs. Rabbit. "We had a basket of blueberries that we picked on Blueberry Hill. I set it on Mrs. Duck's wagon while we were talking. But what does that have to do with Mrs. Duck's eggs?"

Duckworth scooped up Mibs and Dibs, one under each wing, and said, "The last clue—Mibs and Dibs!"

Then he explained. "Mibs and Dibs do everything their mother tells them. If she wants a pillow, they both bring pillows. If she wants a plate of cookies, they both bring plates of cookies. If she wants them to carry a basket of blueberries..."

"They both carry baskets of blueberries," cried Squirrel.

"But there was only one basket of blueberries," said Mrs. Duck.

"Yes," said Duckworth, "but there was another basket with a little pink blanket covering what was inside. So Mibs and Dibs must have thought it was another basket of blueberries."

"I told the children to bring the basket when we left Mrs. Duck," said Mrs. Rabbit. "Each of them must have each picked up a basket. I wasn't paying any attention. When we got home, I told them to put the basket in the pantry."

Detective Duckworth led the way into the pantry.

There it was—Mrs. Duck's basket, with the little pink blanket. It was next to the basket of blueberries.

Duckworth rushed over and peeked under the little pink blanket.

"Aha! The eggs aren't here," he said. "I should have known."

"But four little ducklings <u>are</u>!"
Mrs. Duck was so happy, she couldn't speak.
"Detective Duckworth to the rescue," cried
Squirrel.